AN INFINITE CREATION

Chronicles
of
Temptation

JAZZMINIQUE MOBLEY

Published by Temptation 216
Printed in the United States of America

DEDICATION

THIS BOOK IS DEDICATED TO ALL OF MY
SUPPORTERS. THANK YOU FOR NOT ONLY GETTING
TO KNOW TEMPTATION BUT ALSO GETTING TO
KNOW JAZZMINIQUE.

.

CONTENTS

ACKNOWLEDGMENTS

First and foremost, I would like to thank God for my many blessings. The power of prayer has made a huge impact on my life. Thank you for blessing me with the ability to put my life and creativity into writing.

To my Family, Thanks for the unconditional love and support. Y'all remind me how proud you are of me and I can honestly say I'm just as proud myself. Thank you.

Ivy Lee my fellow Author, my fellow Cancer. Thank you for all of your help. From reading over my work, editing my work, putting me on to everything you know. Taking time out of your day to help me make my dream come true while still maintaining yours. I appreciate you so much.

All my supporters. You have motivated me in more ways than you'll ever know. I needed those "How's the book coming along?" "When the book drop?" "Can't wait to read your book" messages. You all kept me focus and on my shit. I needed that and I love you for that.

C.J. Blaine, Beth, Alexandria, Ashley (Red) thank you for being such amazing friends. I'm always good for telling y'all my stories and now I'm writing them. You all have always been supportive of whatever I've done. I'm blessed to have such genuine and good friends in my life. I love y'all 'til infinity.

Tot (Bestie) we've been girls for over 15 years. No matter the distance, communication, it never affected our friendship/ relationship. You've watched me blossom from a girl into a woman. You literally watched me go from the dorky girl at JFK to one of the hottest bitches in the city. Witnessed such a great, humble transformation and never changed on me. Thank you and I love you.

Tim! Boyyyyyy there were times I was being lazy and out of nowhere you'd ask, "How's the book coming?" and I'll get up and get on it. Thank you! I needed that! You encouraged me so much and checked up on me from the first page 'til the last. Thank you for believing in me.

Brandon, thank you for reading my book and giving me honest feedback. You pumped me up so much had me feeling like "THIS THE ONE" and that I can do anything I put my mind to. You supported me to the fullest. I appreciate you.

Danny (DB) you've been telling me to write a book for YEARS…as long as it took me, I FINALLY did. Thank you for being so encouraging & motivating me TO GET ON IT! You're genuine, kindhearted soul & forever have a place in my life.

@Itstheref thank you for designing my book cover. Most importantly thank you for being professional and easy to work with. Appreciate you to the fullest.

3 Way

I did not know how this was going to play out.

Chase was bringing his baby mama, Ari, to the club tonight. I have never seen her in person only on social media.

For some reason, I just always felt like she was taking shots at me, it's like she knew we was fucking around but she had no proof.

I have been fucking with Chase for over a year now. I met him at the strip club I was dancing at. I knew he had a baby mama, a few to be exact, but it didn't matter to me. Shit, it's rare to find a man with no kids let alone just one. It wasn't like we were in a relationship. We were just kicking it heavy & having some amazing sex.

He hit me up earlier in the day saying they were coming out to the club tonight for Ari's cousin's birthday. Chase told me that Ari has asked him about us multiple times.

He never downplayed his relationship with her; always kept it solid with me. They would be on that on and off and back and forth shit. I was cooling, enjoying being single and entertaining who or whatever I wanted.

Chase stood 6'0 with nice chocolate, smooth skin. Skin so clear it always looks like he is glowing. Teeth just straight as can be, nigga was so black when he smiled in a dark room all you seen was his teeth. That smile would brighten up a bitch day.

Dreads down to his waist. Just as handsome as he can be. As back-and-forth as I was about the gym, he stayed in that bitch. He had to work out at least 6 times a week. The shit paid off, his body was so toned and muscular and he kept himself well groomed.

He could be in some sweats and J's or some slacks and loafers the nigga was still fly. I loved being around him. His energy, his spirit, his conversation, his presence just made me so happy and comfortable. It felt like I had the right person at the wrong time.

I was at work getting dressed and he text me that they are on their way. I usually do not wear make up at work because I have clear and nice skin; besides putting makeup on is too time consuming. As long as my hair, nails and feet did I'm good. But tonight, was a different story.

I had my girl Peaches do my makeup. Peaches

2

was such a raw ass makeup artist. I told her she should take it more seriously. But, between school, 2 kids and dancing she didn't have the time. I come across a lot of single mothers in the dance game with talent.

"Bitch you must have someone special coming up in here tonight for you to get your makeup did," Peaches said jokingly.

I laughed. "Why you say that?"

"Dream, you *never* wear makeup and when you do it's only for some type of event. And ain't shit going on tonight."

I could feel myself beginning to blush.

"So, what swig you got coming in here and please tell me he bringing friends."

I was really private with my personal life when it came to my coworkers. Peaches and I were cool, but I still kept to myself.

I laughed it off. "Yeah, he's bringing friends and they're on their way so hurry up. We got money to make!"

I was procrastinating as I'm making my way upstairs to the VIP section. I'm lightweight nervous because I don't know how this gone go. Chase was worried about her possibly questioning me.

That should've been the least of his worries, I don't owe her no explanation, I'm playing it how you playing it baby.

I was just hoping this won't turn out to be awkward let alone physical. He didn't seem like the type of guy who even dealt with bitches who like to argue and fight but I'm not putting shit past it. I mean, I am fucking her baby daddy.

As I was walking towards the bar there's a crowd of people ordering drinks and of course I instantly lock eyes with Chase.

He was standing there just looking fine as fuck. My pussy always felt like it had a heartbeat when I see him. As excited as I was to see him, I still had to play it off.

As I'm approaching the bar he's conversing with a woman, her back was towards me. She stood about 5'5, wearing a yellow tight skinned dressed, very thick and proportioned and ass was super fat. Hair was styled in a short blonde bob.

If this is Ari I'm thinking in my head, "Damn

she nice" and I'm only seeing her from the back.

"Hey y'all welcome to, "Futures" I said making sure I greeted everyone with a warm welcome.

I hated going to strip clubs and the dancers do not speak let alone introduce themselves. First impressions are the best impressions. In the dance game sometimes, it wasn't always about dancing.

Like you will get money for sitting there talking to someone; fuck a dance your conversation alone can get you paid. And it's not no fake conversation.

I have met a lot of cool people at the club just by us interacting on some talking shit. There's been times they come to the club and not spend a dollar on me and my conversation never changed.

It wasn't always about money. There's been times I needed a male's perspective and sometimes they needed a woman's perspective from me. Men are more comfortable confiding in an entertainer because they feel as though we are going to keep it real. They are more open with us when it comes to dealing with woman. What they'll talk to us about they won't talk to the average woman about.

"Heyyyyyyyy y'all "I said in a cheerful tone as

I hugged a few familiar faces they came with.

I make my way around to speak to everyone then I head towards Chase and Ari. Just as I am walking up Ari and I lock eyes.

She's just as pretty in person. The blonde bob blended so well with her golden skin. The yellow tight dress complimented her figure. Not sure if she does her own make up or not but it was perfect. Since we're locking eyes, I figured I speak to her before I spoke to Chase.

I waved. "Hey I'm Dream."

"Hey I'm Ari" she replied.

Usually when I greet a female customer I shake her hand or give her a hug but this was kind of awkward so I played it from a distance. At this point, Chase is arm length away from me. I figured he was just watching how we interacted with each other.

"What you drinking?" Ari asked.

"Hennessy with a side of coke," I said without having to think twice about it.

"Have you been here before?" I asked.

"Nah this my first time. Today my cousin's birthday and she wanted to hit the strip club. Heard this was a nice spot so we came here." she sips her drink.

"Wassup? We taking shots?" Chase yelled while walking towards us.

I glanced up to see that fine ass smile, smiling back at me.

Ari finishes the rest of her drink, slams the glass on the bar, "Let's go. More shots!"

For some reason I just knew this was about to be a long night. Ari's peoples came in ready to spend money.

Peaches was right up there getting it with me. That's what I liked and respected about her. Bitch was always about her money. She came to work and did her thing and her side hustle would be doing other dancers make up. Shit she just made sixty dollars off doing mine.

It was towards the end of the night and the DJ was slowing the music down.

"Dream give me a dance." Ari surprisingly says.

For some reason I just had to clarify that she just said that.

I gave a surprised expression, "You said you want a dance?"

She giggles, "Yeah c'mon" grabbing my hand leading me to the couch.

As I'm walking with her, I look back at Chase with piercing eyes as he takes another shot of Hennessy.

The DJ just put-on Rihanna's, "Sex with Me" this was like the perfect timing and funny out of all the songs this one?

"Now take it easy on me" she teased.

I offered a smile in gratification.

"I got you." I assured her as I slowly take off the top to my outfit.

Ari scoots further back on the couch to get more comfortable. As she's staring me down from head to toe. I gently began swaying my hips and caressing my breast. I didn't know if she was trying to find a flaw or was somewhat flattered by me. But her eyes never left me.

I climbed on top of her with my breast slightly touching her shoulder while my ass was arched just enough for her to see it while sitting back. She grabs my waist with both hands as I proceed to bounce my ass up and down.

Money begins hitting my body, I look back to

see Chase with a stack of singles. Seeing my ass spread and bouncing on Ari had to turn him on. Chase loved fucking me from the back and all I was thinking about was how I'd take all that dick just like this.

"Ladies and Gentlemen, it's last call, drink up and get your dances. This is last call" DJ Quikz announces on the mic.

"Bae give me some money" Ari reaches her hand out.

Chase hands her the rest of the money in his hand and sits on the couch right in front of us. It was like having a front row seat.

I make my way down to Ari's face, my nipples slightly hard while I'm rubbing my breast along hers.

I slowly placed her right hand on my ass and used my other hand to spread my other cheek. I wanted her to feel how soft and nice my ass was. I could feel her trickle the money down the crack of my ass.

This shit was starting to turn me on.

As I'm dancing on Ari, I turn forward to sit on her lap and Chase is just sitting back enjoying the show. His eyes head on with mines. This made my pussy throb.

I've always joked about us all having a threesome and as good as its sound Chase highly doubted it. They've never had a threesome let alone been ok with him openly dealing with any other woman besides her.

I'm playing with my breast grinding my ass on Ari's pussy while keeping eye contact with Chase. She's grinding back singing along to the lyrics. I can tell the liquor is kicking in for everybody.

I lean back on Ari, our faces side by side as I'm grinding my ass back and forth. I purposefully take her hands and place them on my breast. My eyes never leave Chase.

I can feel my pussy starting to moisten. I take my hands and place them on Ari's hands as she is caressing my breast reassuring her that that is what I want. I have never given a dance and got horny until tonight.

"Last call" the waitress announces.

I smirked. "Yeah 3 more shots of henny."

"Make 'em doubles then close my tab." Chase responded demandingly.

While I'm dancing on Ari, I catch Chase groping his dick. Just by the vicious look he was giving I could tell he wanted to fuck right then and there.

As I'm rubbing on my breast, I take one hand and slowly guide it down to my thong as Chase cautiously watches every move I make.

I pull my thong to the side revealing to Chase how wet my pussy was getting. Still dancing on Ari, I spread her legs a little wider. Her dress made it hard to dance but Chase was the only who could see us, so she was cool. As I am caressing Ari legs as she caresses my breast. My pussy in direct view just for Chase to see.

"Alright Ladies and gentlemen it's the end of the night, I need all of my dancers in the dressing room. We'll be opened tomorrow. Happy Hour starts at 2. Thanks for coming out tonight once again I need all my dancers in the dressing room."

The waitress rushes to us with our last drinks.

"My bad y'all got super busy. It's $65" she interjected.

"Keep the change. Thanks." Chase hands the waitress a hundred-dollar bill.

I stand up to my feet and proceed to put my top back on. Ari gets up as well, fixing her hair along with her dress.

"Last round. Y'all ready?" Ari insisted.

We each grab our drinks, toast, and drink up.

Security approaches us and begin picking up my money putting it in a bag. As I am bending over to help Ari squeezes my ass. Chase is right behind her hands on her waist, biting that sexy ass bottom lip looking like he's about to risk it all. I stop helping security and turn towards them.

"Thanks, y'all, be safe" I hug Ari.

"No problem." as she gives me an even tighter hug.

She scoots towards the side as if she's acknowledging it's ok to hug Chase as well. I haven't touched him all night just been eye fucking like crazy.

We embrace each other with a hug. I made sure to run my tongue along his ear. Ari grabs Chase hand and they head downstairs. Damn I didn't want this night to end.

The night is over and I'm heading towards my car and my phone ring. I knew it was Chase he had his own ringtone whenever he texted or called. It was a text.

"Sup where you at?"

I anxiously replied, "Leaving work just got in the car."

"Pull up to the gas station right up the street from ya job."

I knew exactly what gas station he was talking about. I was wondering if Ari was still with him or not. If she is what is the odds of me pulling up? What if there was an argument after they left? I knew Chase wouldn't had asked me to come up there if there was a problem. He would've just hit me the next day. I started making my way towards the gas station.

I pull up there is a few cars parked with people just standing around not even getting gas. This little gas station be going at night. Usually if it is beef after work, we come up here and fight.

I wasn't surprised it was packed because it was a nice night out. It was four in the morning and it had to be at least 70 degrees outside. It was so warm and relaxing.

I get out of the car.

As the slight wind brushed upon my skin, I hear a female voice yell, "Tracy come here."

I wasn't sure who was calling me especially by my real name. That was super rare. I follow the voice to find Ari standing by the gas pump. Not sure where

Chase was because I know he's not making her pump the gas.

With folded arms I asked, "I know you not pumping gas?" As I made my way towards her.

"Girl hell nah, I needed some air, that damn Hennessy fucking with me. Plus, Chase went inside to get some Backwoods."

We both laughed it off. Suddenly, there's a slight pause.

Ari begins coming closer to me, we are literally faced to face. Paying no mind that we are out in the open, without a word we begin kissing. I held her face gently as she held mine. We play tag with each other's tongues. She kissed me with such passion, I damn near felt like I could orgasm right then and there.

I pulled away at the sudden intensity.

She ignored me as she came even closer and begin rubbing her hand in between my thighs. My plan was to shoot straight home after work and shower, so I didn't bother putting any panties on.

Her touch was so persuasive and seductive I could feel my pussy juices slowly coming down. She rubbed her fingers up and down my clit, while slowly easing a finger inside me. A soft groan breaks loose at the sudden pleasure. Just when I was making my way to play with her pussy my phone ring.

It's Chase.

"You here? I'm inside grabbing Backwoods".

As disappointed as I was that his text interrupted us, I was kind of happy. Shit was getting intense. I wanted to eat Ari's pussy so bad while Chase fucked me from the back.

"Yeah, I'm here outside talking to Ari" I texted back.

Chase slightly jogs his way to the car. As he's making his way Ari whispers, "You coming with us?"

I placed her fingers in my mouth sucking my pussy juices off, I whispered back, "Am I?"

Ari suggested that we keep the party going so I got in my car and followed behind them. This shit was crazy to me. I went the whole day worrying about if things would go wrong and everything was cool.

I know Chase had to be just as shocked; watching both of your bitches getting along is quite the flex and with Ari being the one to suggest we keep it going made it feel more comfortable. I knew she knew that we've been fucking.

Did curiosity kill the cat?

I used to always joke to Chase about us having a threesome and he would say Ari never been with a woman she ain't with that.

Yet here we are.

We pull up to The Hilton in Beachwood. I gather my things making sure I grab lotion, deodorant, and spray from my dance bag I absolutely needed to take a shower. I get out the car and make my way towards them. Ari had a bottle of Moët in one hand and a blunt in the other.

"You smoking?" she asked passing me the blunt.

"Hell yeah."

Inhaling the exotic kush down my throat. Chase makes his way around the car to hit the blunt, sneaking a grab at my ass while doing so. Holding a bottle of 1800 silver, I could tell this was about to be a long and fun night.

The room was nice I could tell they got ready here before coming to the club, room smelt just like his cologne. Chase had his own scent like if anybody else in the world wore that scent, I'd think of him.

"Mind if I take a shower?" I asked.

"Go ahead there's extra towels in the bathroom." Ari insisted.

"Aye before getting in take this." Chase said handing me a shot of 1800.

We all raise our drinks in the air.

"What we toasting to?" I asked while looking at Ari.

"To a good night" she replied.

"To a good night "we sang in unison.

The shower I took was everything. Felt so fresh and clean; much needed when you've been dancing all night and different people touching all over you. Dancing all over the stage will have you scrubbing your body down.

They had the music going not too loud but loud enough. I was debating on should I come out naked or at least put something on, I didn't know what was going on out there. What if I came out there and they were fucking?

I wrapped the towel around my waist and come out. There were three glasses of my Moët sitting on the dresser.

Chase and Ari were in the other shower I could hear the water running. I was surprised they didn't hop in with me. I was assuming they were just respecting my privacy and if this was going to be the night that I thought it was then the shower is where we can end up at.

I helped myself to one of the glasses and in doing so they were just coming out from their shower.

Right on time.

I noticed they were also wrapped in towels as I pass them each a glass.

We toast once again.

"Your night at work was cool?" Ari asked.

"Hell yeah, great night. Thanks to y'all."

"You feel like dancing? We still have singles." She asked.

I don't know if this was her way to getting it started or not because Chase wasn't saying anything he was just going with the flow.

I absolutely did not mind getting some more money and dancing for them in private. I started to ask if she wanted me to put on a dance outfit with heels, but I wasn't about to go through all that.

Let's cut the games get straight to the point.

Ari sat on the edge of the bed while Chase sat in the lounge chair right across from us. With his champagne glass in one hand and the bottle of 1800 in another, he was looking as if he was preparing to watch a good ass movie.

Drakes *Shut It Down* began playing. Chase knew I loved this song, sang it to him so much that I know he had to think of me every time he hears it.

I was facing towards him with my back towards Ari as I drop my towel. I wanted straight eye contact with him as he watched two of his favorite bitches.

He began to put his drink down and reaches in his pants pockets and pull out a stack of singles and begin throwing them.

As I am dancing on Ari, I can see his dick rising up through the towel. Bringing my focus back to Ari I turn around to face her; slowly moving my hips and caressing my breast.

I could tell Ari was getting turned on she begin touching herself as well. Before you know it, her towel was off.

Her body was just as nice as mine.

Nice big titties, flat stomach, nice fat ass. She begins sucking on my titties one at a time. I was turned on; I could feel my pussy starting to get wet.

As we were slowly falling back onto the bed, I get on top of her. Sliding my tongue into her mouth while my ass poked up in the air for Chase to get a view of how wet my pussy was.

He throws more money.

"Baby get over here." She demands.

Without hesitation Chase makes his way over towards us. Ari lets out a slight groan. He wasted no time going inside her.

With her legs lifted Chase begin stroking her pussy while holding my hips as Ari and I kissed. Her moans begin to get louder and louder.

He pulls out and as he does, I come down to taste Ari while he put his manhood inside me as I ate her.

Chase was pounding my pussy as I sucked on Ari. She tasted so good and he felt so good, spreading my ass making sure I felt every stroke.

I was bent over on the edge of the bed with pussy in my mouth and dick inside me; it took me to complete ecstasy.

The moaning of satisfaction between them both was so intriguing. With me making my pussy muscles go in and out made him go harder.

Suddenly, I begin squirting all over the floor. It literally sounded like a waterfall.

Chase pulls out.

As bad as I wanted him to stay inside me, I knew he had to bring his focus back on to Ari. The last thing he would want to do is make her upset. You always have to give the main bitch more attention in a threesome.

I stand up and proceed to watch them. I suddenly begin to feel a little funny. Like my body felt different. I wasn't sure if it was the liquor or the champagne, but I wasn't feeling the same. I did not want to ruin the mood, so I play it off like I had to use the bathroom.

I rush towards the bathroom and begin throwing water on my face to cool me down for some reason I was feeling extremely hot.

What the fuck is going on?

I give it a few minutes then go back out.

I was playing it cool I go back out. Chase is standing on the edge of the bed while Ari's sucking him off. Although I wasn't feeling my best I was still turned on and wanted to keep going.

I joined her as I place his balls in my mouth while she kept on sucking. She gently grabs my face and she places his manhood inside of my mouth.

I wanted Ari to feel like she had the control. I mean that is the least I can do since he and I have been fucking on the low so long.

We take turns sucking him off and at one point we even sucked him together. Both of our tongues going up and down enjoying the taste of our juices. I was ready to get fucked.

"Let's take a shot." Ari insisted.

Deep down inside I really didn't want to take a shot. That champagne was kicking my ass on the low. I think the liquor made her more relaxed. She gets up and begin pouring shots.

"Damn I kind of feel funny." I said.

Letting out a slight giggle Chase says "I put some molly in the champagne."

"Whaaaaaaaaatttt?!" Ari yells.

Damn this explains why I feel how I feel.

"I only put a little bit in there baby."

Now I've popped a pill or two in my life, so I really wasn't tripping but he could've told us. I assumed they did it before as well because she wasn't mad or tripping either. But we dead ass needed water.

Luckily, I brought some up from my car that were in my dance bag. I only had two, so I kept one for myself and gave them the other.

"This my last shot." I said jokingly but was serious.

The water cooled me down and I was ready to finish what we started. We began making our way back to the bed and I lay on the bed spreading my legs.

Following behind me Ari puts her face right in between them. I know for a fact she has never eaten pussy before and that she has never gotten her pussy ate by a woman. I wasn't expecting the best head, but I didn't mind guiding her either.

Chase begins hitting her from the back while she ate me while he and I looked each other in the eyes the whole time. I was so turned on watching him fucking her.

Ari was actually doing a good job eating me out. Although this was her first time, a woman knows what a woman wants. Maybe she was eating my pussy the way she likes hers ate. Regardless the shit was hitting.

I proceeded to get up making sure Ari stays in doggy style position. As she's bent over, I spread her ass open for Chase.

"Fuck her." I demanded.

I began to bring my face closer to his and as he goes in and out, I begin devouring his tongue. Grabbing Ari ass to help her throw it back on his dick. She moaned in complete satisfaction.

"Damnnnnnn bae."

Bringing my focus to Ari, "Feel good don't it?"

That was a silly question considering she been fucking him for years and we both know it's good. But the talking during sex just made it so much freakier and turned me on.

"Take all that dick" I insisted while spreading her ass open a little more.

She begins to throw it back even harder as if she no longer needed my assistance. I let her throw it back a few more times then pull him out of her. I wanted to taste her on his dick.

Chase holds my head and guides me to sucking. I stop and place him back inside her. I was feeling the molly more than ever now.

Then out of nowhere Chase says, "Bae I wanna tell you I've been fucking her the whole time."

Slightly pausing.

Did this nigga really just say that?

Like here?

Right now?

This just really can't be happening. This damn sure wasn't the time or the place.

Everything stops. Ari turns the music down.

"Chase I'm not no dumb bitch, I been knew you was fucking her. It's just silly as fuck you would say that right now."

"I know baby I'm just lightweight geeked and wanted to get the shit off my chest."

They were dead ass having this conversation in front of me as if I wasn't standing right there. I wasn't sure where this was going and wasn't sure if I should stay or leave.

Chase really killed the mood with this one. If molly, make you confess to some shit then maybe you shouldn't take it. I started gathering my things because it started getting awkward. This was a conversation they needed to have in private.

"Wasup where you going?" Ari asked.

"Y'all having a serious conversation right now and I'm not trying to be in the middle of it."

"Girl bye it's too late you've been in the middle. We're already here the shit is in the air. We gone finish what we started. Chase we'll talk about this shit later."

Chase was sitting on the edge of the bed looking about lost as fuck. His dick was still on hard though. He started this conversation and suddenly was quiet. I'm assuming that he was lightweight regretting saying anything, but it was too late.

Just when I was thinking *So what now?* Ari begins sucking him off and I join her. This time she makes me get on top as she rode his face in reverse making sure she and I were face to face.

"Ride that dick," she commands.

I begin whining my hips as Ari tongue is down my throat. My pussy was so wet. I used my pussy muscles to grip Chase dick. I knew that shit turned him on and would make him cum. But I wasn't about to let him.

One thing about a threesome that nut have to come from the main bitch otherwise there goes another argument. It's one thing for a woman to share her man and watch him get complete pleasure for another but that nut, that nut goes to her.

I could tell he was about to bust, so I hop off and bring Ari head to his dick. I wanted to see if she will swallow or spit. As she sucked, I jacked.

Ari grabs my head to join her. As I jacked Chase begins to moan in contentment.

"I'm about to bussssssssssst."

I began jacking him harder as she licked his balls. Warm nut begins shooting all over our face.

Shit was so intense.

We couldn't swallow or spit, so we just kissed as the nut ran down our faces. This was my second threesome, and it was so much better than my first.

I fulfilled a fantasy that Chase thought was impossible. I was Ari's first female sexual encounter. I loved Chase but I'm sure I didn't love him the same way she did and I'm sure she didn't love him the way I did.

We end the night with a group shower. Getting into bed Chase lays in between us. This nigga must've felt like *the* man and if so, I'm glad he did.

That is how I wanted him to feel.

BIRTHDAY SPECIAL

Raymell's birthday was today and I was contemplating on what to do. Shopping for men has always been a hard task for me. Going all the way back from birthdays and Father's Day with my father; from getting him cologne to tool kits.

I know he had to lightweight be tired of the shit, but hey it was the thought that count. Raymell only wore one specific cologne that he had enough of, so that was out the question. I learned never to buy a man shoes he'll walk out your life in them, so that was definitely out of the question.

He wasn't materialistic at all so buying him some expensive clothing or jewelry would've been more like a waste to him. Plus, he works so much he never really take time out to do anything.

I said to myself, "Man let me FaceTime Tee and ask him."

Tee was my best friend known him since we were in diapers. His mom and my mom were best friends and were pregnant with us at the same time, so we practically grew up together.

From Preschool to High School we have been inseparable. We were so close that people would mistake us for being brother and sister or even think that we were dating. We had more of a brother and sister type of bond.

As cute as a *Love & Basketball* story sounds, we never took it there. I loved having a best friend of the opposite sex. Whenever I needed advice from a male perspective I called on Tee, just like I'm about to do right now.

"Yooooooooooooooo" Tee shouted.

He was at the barbershop getting a haircut which explains why he was so loud.

"Awwwwwww shit I see you boyyyyyyyyyyy fresh cut" I shouted back.

Laughing it off, "Sup with you?"

"Shit, trying to figure out what to get Ray for his birthday. Any suggestions?" I anxiously asked.

Wiping the hair off his face he looks into the camera and give me the slightest grin.

"Aye it's getting cold outside make him a gift basket. Socks, boxers, scarf. His job does involve working outside so something like that."

Smacking my lips. "Mannnnnn you don't think that's jake?"

He paused. "Man what? Hell, nah that's something he's going to need. And it's really about the thought that count as well. Men don't be all into birthday gifts and shit. To have a woman that take time to show any type of appreciation is cool."

That lightweight made me feel kind of better. It didn't have to take a birthday, holiday any special occasion for me to show Raymell I cared.

I'd do something as random as sending an Edible Arrangement to his job, cash app him haircut money for his weekly cut, book us massage appointments on a random day.

If he didn't work so hard shit, we could've gone out the country. He has been nothing but good to me and I didn't mind showing my appreciation. I'm sure whatever I decide he'll be appreciative.

"Aight cool. I'm about to run a few errands. Hit you back a little later I love you, thanks."

Admiring his new cut, "No problem love you too talk to you later."

I make my way to T.J. Maxx. I grab a pack of boxer briefs, thermals, socks, razors, clippers. He was a big fan of the *Cleveland Browns* football team so, when I came across a Browns blanket, hat, and coffee mug I had to get it. I was just grabbing everything he could possibly like, need and/or use putting it in my cart.

Afterwards, I stopped at another store to grab a gift bag and a birthday card. Before heading in I wanted to stop by a florist shop. Why not add some sexiness to the celebration? I needed rose petals. As goofy and silly as I was, I could still be sexy.

Finally, home after all that running around. Although I had to work tonight, I made sure to tell Ray to come over before I had to go in.

I would have cooked dinner, but time wasn't looking so good plus Ray was linking with some friends before coming to me. I begin setting everything up. Putting all his gifts inside a big birthday bag along with a card. Bought one of the biggest birthday balloons tied it to the bag.

As I placed everything on the bed, I realized I have tea light candles. I grabbed a few, aligning them along the wall, from the entrance door all the way to my bedroom. I figured I'd do my make up I had to work anyways, and I really wanted to look my best and be sexy for him tonight. Suddenly, my phone rings.

"Babe!" Ray aggressively yell.

I could tell he was at the bar. Music was super loud and by the looks of it the liquor was kicking in.

We both decided to chill out on our drinking, but I knew today was an exception especially if he was linking with his boys.

"I'm about to be on my way." He insisted.

I paused. "I hope you're not driving."

Ray eyes were bloodshot red. His words were slurring as he was talking to me. I stayed about 30 minutes from where he was at, there was no way he was going to drive from there to my house. I didn't want to be selfish, but I was kind of disappointed. I felt like on his birthday he should have spent some time with me.

It's amazing how people don't ever support you or come out until it's a birthday or a funeral. The next time he hears from half these people will be his next birthday.

Wiping the sweat off his face, "
I'm......I'm...... I'm....going to get dropped off to you. I'm staying the night while you're at work."
I sighed." Ok, be careful. I have to be at work in a few hours so try to hurry up babe if not we can link tomorrow."

As considerate as that sounds, I didn't mean it. I wanted to see him tonight. My whole vibe was on some chill, sexy, and romantic shit. I had music playing, candles lit, lingerie on. I wanted to see my man!

"Aight see you shortly." I said through gritted teeth.

Thirty minutes turned into an hour; an hour turned into two. I had to be to work in less than an hour and he still wasn't here. Like what the fuck is taking so long? I decided to call him back.

Slightly rolling my eyes. "Damn you know I have to be at work, like wassup?"

"Babe, leave your keys outside I'll be there when you get off."

I was speechless.

I don't know how much liquor he had but wasn't no way in hell I was going to leave my keys outside. He was even more out of it than before.

At this point I'm actually mad. Why couldn't I get your time on such a special day? Why couldn't you link with your boys after you seen me? Did you really have to get so drunk?

My eyes welled up with tears then I hung up on him and proceeded to get ready for work. I was disappointed and hurt.

Throughout the night I didn't get not one call or text. It was weird to me because no matter how intoxicated I was I always reached out to him.

Shit sucked.

I could barely focus at work because I was so irritated. I decided to send him a video and pics of me in my lingerie, the candles just the whole set up. It's not that I wasted my time or money, it's just that I wanted to show him something different that a celebration doesn't mean you have to get drunk. I've never done nothing like this for a man, so it was different for me. And for him not to show up had me furious.

It's the end of the night still no call or text. You mean to tell me all these hours went by and you haven't checked your phone at all? I make my way home.

As I'm driving home, I'm talking all kinds of shit to myself. Practicing what I'm going to say to him once he does call. All I know is that he wasn't getting not one more text or call from me. I make it home, shower and take my ass to bed. Few hours into my sleep there's a knock on my door.

I get out the bed, grab my robe and make my way to the door. Looking out the peephole it's Ray in his pajamas. I'm assuming he just came straight from his house. All that shit talking I was saying to myself somehow went out the window. I was still excited to see him but still had to act somewhat upset.

Although, I was still feeling some kind of way, I still wanted to be around him. Without a word I ajar the door and make my way back to the bed. Throwing the cover over me positioning myself to get back comfortable.

In an apologetic voice, "Man babe I'm sorry I got too fucked up. As soon as I woke up, I made my way to you."

I looked over at Ray, "I'm salty as fuck cause I dead ass told you first thing this morning to make sure that I seen you. And for you to say that you are on your way and it takes two hours was so inconsiderate."

I fluff my pillow to get comfy and turn my head. Ray proceeded to make his way towards the bed.

"I know I'm not getting that fucked up again. You know how that goes one drink turn into ten. Everybody kept buying me drinks."

"You don't know your limit?" I interrupted.

Smacking his lips, "Now c'mon you know I haven't been drinking so that shit hit a little different and it's my birthday you know how that shit goes."

With my back turned towards him he crawls into bed lying beside me. Gently wrapping his hand around my waist, placing a kiss on my neck.

"Don't be mad at me." He whispered.

I wasn't as furious as a few hours ago. I was actually cool. I just really wanted him to understand how I felt. I didn't feel like I was a priority on such a special day for him. I can't imagine not seeing him on my birthday especially if he had let me know that he wanted to see me earlier that morning.

Rolling over to look at him, "I got all dressed up, music playing, candles lit, makeup did and felt like a complete fool because you didn't show up. Dude I cried for like 3 minutes."

With a slight grin. "Aye! Go put that lingerie back on." he said.

Rolling my eyes "Nope it's not the same. I done wiped my makeup off, my hair wrapped now. The mood not even the same."

"Aye go put that lingerie on." He demanded.

I did as he said. The way he was talking to me was lightweight turning me on. There's no point of us going back-and-forth what's done is done, he's here now so, make the best of it.

I get out the bed and go to my drawer. I had this purple and black lingerie dress that I never wore before and totally forgot I even had. My breast filled the lace so perfectly. There was a slight opening on the right side that revealed my thigh and damn near my pussy.

"Now go light the candles." He insisted.

The tea light candles that were already on the floor had gone out from waiting on him earlier. I grabbed new ones out my kitchen drawer along with a lighter. On my hands and knees, I begin to light each candle. As I am lighting the candles Ray gets on the floor with me.

Before I could light the candle, I feel Ray fingers sliding along my pussy lips. My ass was tooted in the air, with my dress slenderly above my waist, while my pussy is slightly showed from the back. Me bending over lightning the candles must have turned him on.

He eased his fingers inside of me while placing a gentle kiss on each of my ass cheeks. I gasp as his tongue caressed my clit. Getting head from the back was a different type of feeling.

"Light all them candles" he importuned.

I did as he said. I could feel my pussy juices dripping down my thigh. Not to toot my own horn, but I had some of the wettest pussy a nigga could ever fuck. I'm talking dripping all the way from my pussy down to my ass.

Ray was an ass man and I had more than enough. Before I could even reach a slight orgasm, Ray puts the tip of his dick in me.

"I said light the candles." Sounding even more demanding.

I grab the lighter and light the first candle. Ray filled my body with soft thrushes working every inch of himself inside of me.

I was crawling, lightning candles and getting fucked from the back, talk about multitasking. For every candle I lit every stroke I get. We are down to the last candle, I stand up walk towards the bed Ray follows.

Laying on the bed with my legs spread apart I began to play with myself. Using my right hand to play with my pussy using my left hand to caress my nipples.

Ray stood before me, dick hard just admiring me pleasuring myself. As he's watching me, he slowly strokes his dick, my pussy is getting even more wet. It turned me on watching him jack off in front of me. I lift up and crawl towards him placing his long, thick dick in my mouth. Staring him dead in the eyes while devouring his dick down my throat.

"Damn bae" Ray slightly moan.

Ray liked sloppy head. I'm talking spit all on his dick all the way to his balls. My mouth was so wet, but my pussy was even wetter. I wasn't letting Ray get this nut off in my mouth I wanted to get fucked.

Lifting my face up, he proceeds to play tag with my tongue. I absolutely loved kissing it was one of my favorite signs of affection. I never understood how people can have great sex and not kiss.

Without a word, I turn over and bend my ass over placing his dick right in between my pussy lips. With my face down on the mattress and ass up, I spread my legs slimly, wide enough to grab his dick from in between my thighs and rub it along my pussy. Enduring the pleasure of my pussy being teased, I place the tip of his dick inside me.

Ray filled my body with soft thrusts, working every inch inside of me. Spreading my ass open as he rotated his hips in gentle motion.

"Not yet," he whispered.

Ray knew my body so well. He must have felt my pussy muscles throbbing. That's how he always knew I was about to cum. My pussy would tighten up on his dick. As bad as I wanted to hold it in I just couldn't.

"I can't babe I'm about to cum." I moaned. With my face down, I take my hands and spread my ass open.

"Fuck me." I demanded.

Ray gives me deeper and harder strokes. My ass clapping louder and louder the harder he goes. I keep my ass spread open to show him I'm taking all that dick.

"Harder! Harder! Give me all that dick." I begged.

"You want that dick? You want that dick?"

I can feel Rays dick throbbing the harder he goes. That nut was coming, and I was ready to catch it wherever he decided to put it.
"Aaaaaaaahhhhh." He screamed in such pleasure.
I was having my own orgasm as well while he unloaded his nut right inside of me. Pacing ourselves

he pulls out. I can feel his nut trickling down my thighs.

Laying there on my stomach in such ecstasy, Ray come lay beside me placing soft kisses on my back. Within a few minutes he was sleep.

"Happy Birthday Baby."

.

FATAL ATTRACTION

I can't remember what we were arguing about, but I brushed it off and went into his room.

He had just moved into his new spot and I don't like to argue or being loud especially when you live in an apartment, the neighbors be in your business.

I lay in the bed watching TV and he comes into the room close the door and begin closing the blinds. My gut feeling was telling me something wasn't right. I was done with the argument but for some reason he would not let it go.

He closes the blinds then begin to turn the TV up real loud as if he didn't want anyone to hear us. Now my heart is pounding and he's giving me this look.

As I'm lying in the bed, I'm naked. He's also naked. We were always walking around the house naked. So, he stands in front of the TV with this devilish look on his face. I can never forget how his face would scrunch up, eyes become so little, jaws lock up and you could just see the anger in his face.

He gets on the bed and just stares at me. In my head I'm just asking God, *why did I come back over here?*

All we did was argue.

Drugs had him so fucked up that he was paranoid. Accusing me of sleeping with the neighbors. Accusing me of being at the apartment on certain nights and I would be at home.

One time he even text me talking about he can hear me next door; I was dead ass at home. I lived about 20 minutes away from him.

So, he is standing in front of the tv then walks around the bed towards my way and instantly get on top of me.

As he laid on top of me, he began to choke me and say things like, "I'm tired of you playing with me."

I kept telling him to get off me but that didn't matter. As he is on top of me, he rams his dick in my ass. Now we've done anal sex before, but this definitely wasn't willingly and was forced.

I was crying and trying to scream but remind you he turned the TV up so loud nobody could really hear me. He lived in apartments where the walls weren't too thin, and you really can't hear too much in others ppl apartments.

If anything, they probably heard how loud the TV was. As he is raping me, he pulls his gun out from under the pillow. He always kept the gun under the pillow.
He became so paranoid that whenever we came in from being out, he would search the whole place as soon as we got inside to make sure nobody was

hiding inside his apartment. That came from when back in the days he would pay a guy who was working at some apartments, to get the key to other people apartments and rob them while they are gone.

Even told me one time someone came home, and he had to hide that's why he became so paranoid about his own place. He pulls the gun out and puts it right by my head as he laid on top of me.

I'm looking him in his face crying and telling him to stop as a gun is pointed to my head while I'm getting raped.

All he kept saying was, "Why do you keep playing with me? Why do you keep playing with me?

This instantly made me think of this episode of, *Fatal Attraction* that I had watched recently. This young lady was woken up to her baby father having a gun to her face because as she slept, he went through her phone and was upset at what he had seen.
He woke her up repeatedly saying, "Why do you keep playing with me?" As I laid in that bed and had those exact words said to me, I cried even harder.

On that episode of *Fatal Attraction,* he shot her in her face. Although, she survived he killed her mother. All I could do was think of that episode I was in the same scenario.

I pleaded and pleaded with him to get the gun out my face. Suddenly, there was this noise in the kitchen.

He hopped up and said, "Did you hear that?"

Of course, it was nothing, but he was so paranoid every little noise made him grab his gun.

And that he did.

Now he is off of me and searching the apartment to see if anyone is hiding. I was so happy that he got distracted. I was able to get up. I leave the room and go to the kitchen. His living room and kitchen was all in one. He had an island countertop as well.

He's searching the extra bedroom. I am naked and scared but I need to get out of this apartment.

As soon as he sees me in the kitchen he says, "What are you doing get back in the room."

I'm playing it off as cool as possible, but my heart pounding and I'm scared as fuck. So, I just act as if I'm grabbing us something to drink. At this point he just can't keep his eyes off of me.

As he's making his way towards me my phone goes off. That also distracts him. He goes in the room grabs my phone it is a lock code on it, and he ask me to open it.

Of course, I'm not about to unlock it. I tell him I want to go home throw me my clothes because I'm not going back into the room. But he insists on me going inside the room.

I refused and by this time I'm on one side of the island and he's on the other. He can't instantly get to me. I'm running around the island trying not to let him get to me.

He couldn't jump over the counter because he had my phone in one hand and the gun in the other. He suddenly begins pleading that he's not going to hurt me and all I'm asking him is to throw me my clothes so I can go.

The front door is right by the kitchen, but the only thing is if I try to run out the door, he has a trash can blocking it. Which means I must be super-fast. He kept a trash can by the front door with plates on top just in case anybody tried to break in at night he would hear them. I'm telling you paranoid as fuck. I absolutely hated living like that.

We are in the kitchen standing across from each other. I'm asking for my phone and to let me go home. He throws my phone expecting me not to be fast enough to grab it before he can get to me. I grabbed that phone so fast and ran to the other side of the island.

Now he is even more irritated and pointing the gun at me. When I tell you, I thought this man was about to kill me. All I wanted to do was make it out that door naked or not I need to get out.

He's in front of me, the refrigerator is right behind me, the door is to my left. I made the run. He chased me to the door as my hand touches the handle, he grabs me but I'm not letting go and I'm screaming as loud as I can.

He still has the gun, and we are fighting over the door. Thank God there were no locks on the door and that the handle was pretty much a push down and door opens. Had it been Locks on the door it would have been even more hard getting out. Or honestly, I probably would have never made it out.

The trash can being in the way was hard enough. We are fighting over the door and the gun drops. It was so loud that I thought it went off, but I didn't care all I wanted to do is get out of there.

Naked with my phone in my hand I run into the hallway.... he started chasing me but the fact he was naked made him run back in.

I ran to elevator, pressed the button then ran around to the corner and stood right in front of an apartment door holding my breath covering my nose.

I knew he would get dressed and come out and he did. I could hear him calling my name in the halls.

My heart was pounding.

I am naked and cold but can't let him hear me. I'm calling my sister hoping she'll pick up just in case he catches me she can hear what's going on. I hear him press the elevator button and he hops on and leave. I gave it a few seconds. I stayed on the phone with my sister.

He's gone.

I hurry up run inside his apartment throw my clothes on, grab my stuff and hit the stairs. I was so relieved to be out.

LOTTERY TICKET

Que and I always played the numbers. After Cleveland built *The Horseshoe Casino* I got more into gambling.

Blackjack was my game.

When I tell you, I could literally flip $100 to $1,000 with no problem. I even got into playing the lottery. And I use to smack the fuck out my numbers.

One thing about me, I've always had a way of attracting money. From my mom buying me a book bag for school that I found money in, to me having to do community service picking up trash on the freeway and finding money.

I got into playing the Ohio lottery playing the pick 3 and pick 4. I would hit very often. I usually played the same numbers but every now and then I would switch it up because I always felt like if I kept seeing a certain number that is my sign to go play it.

I was on my way to my hair appointment. My best friend Ashley birthday was coming up and we were taking a last-minute trip to Las Vegas.

Que wasn't too thrilled especially because we just booked it like not even two days ago. There was always some tension when I wanted to be around my family and friends.

I hated the feeling of wanting to do something instead of having his support it was always an argument. Ashley and I birthdays two weeks apart and we always celebrated together. There was no way I was going to miss this trip even if it cost Que and I an argument.

While on my way to the salon I just kept seeing the number 626. I always play the number as my pick 3 because my birthday is June 26.

I Was running behind on time but figured I would play my number once my hair was done. I'm sitting under the dryer as my hair dry, my phone rings.

"Hey Bae, wassup?"

"I'm around your way do you wanna ride with me to the store to play the numbers?"

"Yeah, I'll go, I'm sitting up under the dryer anyway."
Que pulls up and I hop in. I sat inside the car as he went inside and played the numbers. He knew the numbers I played so he played them for me. He shoots me back to the salon we sat in the car talking and smoking then I headed back in so I can finish up.

The vibe was cool, and everything was good. So, as I am getting my hair did and I check for the winning numbers and 626 came out.

I'm all excited and shit cause every $3 gives you $500 and I usually play $6 so that's an $1000 win.

Considering the fact, I took a last-minute trip to Las Vegas which means I have to miss work which means I'm missing out on money I can use that $1000.

I'm calling Que to tell him but he's not answering. I figured he may have been a little busy, so I gave it a little time. I called back and was texting, and he still wasn't answering. Suddenly, my phone ring.

I answered, "Damn babe I've been hitting you up to tell you 626 came."

Remind you, I'm super excited and done told my beautician and the ladies in the salon how my numbers came out.

Que says in such a negative tone of voice," Yeah, I see."

I'm lightweight lost like I had got this feeling that this was about to be a problem. It's like sharing exciting news with someone who isn't happy for you.

There is a slight pause in the conversation then he says, "You ain't give me no money to play your number."

I'm in disbelief to even hear this nigga say that. We played each other's numbers plenty of time and if the shoe were on the other foot and I paid for his tickets it wouldn't have made a difference. It is $6.00 I have given this man THOUSANDS before. How are we even having this conversation?

"Yeah, I walked in the store and played the numbers."

I yell back, "Nigga my hair wasn't fuckin done and since when we both have to go inside and play?"

Then he hits me with the, "I didn't play your number. "

I was so frustrated and irritated cause he is playing the fuck out of crazy. One minute it is that I didn't give you money to play the numbers so it's yours. The next it was you didn't play my numbers.

Like this nigga knew I was about to go on a trip, he knew I was about to miss out on work, he knew those were my numbers and I play them and he's really about to try to play me for a punk ass thousand dollars?

It's like had it been me I would have been happy for him, would've gave him the tickets. I would have even given him some money off of my win just for playing it. I was leaving tomorrow and as salty as I was, I went on that trip and had the time of my life.

Nigga ain't stop shit!

Now let's fast forward to 3 months later

I don't know what it was about this nigga, but I just couldn't stop fuckin' with him. Our relationship was so unhealthy. Something so toxic that I was losing myself.

I should have been stopped fuckin' with him, but I felt like I could change him. I felt bad that he barely had family, so I welcomed him into mine.

My family perceived him as being a good guy, but he was everything but that. We had our good times but the bad outweighed the good. Yet I kept coming back around.

I wake up get dressed about to go see him at his apartment. While I'm on my way I stop and play my numbers. He texts me ask me to play 411 because he forgot to play while he was out and did not want to leave back out. And of course, I did with no problem.

He told me to put $12 on the number 411. I was surprised he even forgot to play the number because he played it faithfully.

As I am leaving the store headed to his way something told me to keep the tickets inside my car. All I could think about is how he did me. I literally thought of the scenario of me sitting down chilling with him then I check my phone and see that the 411 came.

Then, I bounce on his ass.

As I am pulling up to the apartment I'm really debating on if I should leave the tickets in the car or to bring them up. I would have never had this debate with myself had he not played me that one day at the salon. Although I let it go, I felt some kind of way.

If I leave them in the car and he finds out 411 came we're going to fight our way down to the car until he gets them. If I bring them in the house we're going to be fight inside. Either way there was going to be an argument, so I took my chances with the car. At least we're out in the public, I feel safer.

I get upstairs we are chilling' and watching TV. He is about to get ready to take a shower so as he is doing that something told me to check the numbers.

As God is my witness 411 came.

My heart was pounding so fast because I was happy and nervous. Like I literally thought this whole scenario out and its really happening. He is getting his self together and talking to me while he is doing it.

Now I already know the numbers, but he doesn't, he's not even thinking about it. All I could think about is that I really need to get out of the apartment.

I wasn't giving him those tickets. That same day I had an appointment to get my car looked at. I never told Que the time, so I decided to act as though the mechanic just called me.

I walked inside the bathroom heart pounding because I'm not sure if he's going to believe me. He's in a towel about to hop in the shower and I walk in

"Hey, the mechanic just called me and said I could bring the car now. "

He looks at me with this funny look and says, "Damn so you about to leave right now?"

"Yeah, I mean I'll be back but rather drop it off now get it over with. It's gonna take a few hours."

He just looked at me and surprisingly he said, "Ok."

Maybe it was my guilty conscience the fact that I knew what was going on and he didn't have me nervous as fuck.

As I'm leaving, he walks behind and jokingly says, "Wassup you went in my pockets or something you seem like you're in a rush."

I laughed it off then hurried my ass downstairs in my car and drove off. I just won $2000.
I'm about 15 minutes into my drive and he calls me. I ignore it. It was funny to me like wow look at karma doing its thing.
My phone rings again.

I answer. "Yeah 'sup?"

"Nah you know wassup bring me my tickets. That's why yo' ass left like that" in a jokingly manner.

I hit him with the, "Nahhhhhhh bruh you ain't give me no money on these. Remember when you did that to me?"

"Really? So, this your pay back? Those my tickets you wouldn't had even played them if I didn't tell you."
He got to threatening me and claiming he can sue me. Lol.
Funniest shit ever.
Isn't it funny how the tables turn? Just a couple months ago he did the same exact thing to me. Had

he never done that to me I would have gave him the tickets.

How we in a relationship arguing over money?

He was absolutely right, had he not said that I would've never played but that was my sign and his karma. He went as far as asking me to even split it with him. I Banged on his ass and went to get my car fixed.

Jokes on you.

MIAMI

I was graduating from Ohio Media School in a week. Considering the fact, I never got the chance to walk across stage for my high school graduation, this was such a big deal.

As excited as I was there was a slight disappointment because Jason and I was not on good terms.

We have been dating for about a year in a half now. He had a bad habit of ignoring me when we were going through shit. Even when he was in the wrong, I always caught myself reaching out.

Jason had this rule where no matter how mad or upset we were at each other we don't call each other out each other's name. But this one night I was a little too drunk and extremely heated that it led to me calling him a *bitch ass nigga* and that got me blocked off his phone and all social networks.

Even after sobering up I tried to apologize but he wasn't trying to hear it. He was there for my orientation, so I definitely wanted him to be there for my graduation. But I wasn't going to beg for support. He knew how much this meant to me.

It has been about a month since I have spoken to Jason. Within this time frame I began talking to a childhood friend name Stacey.

I have known him since we were about 10 years old and every now and then he had come to the strip club and show me some love. The fact we knew each other already and kept in touch ever so often made us quite comfortable with one another from jump.

Stacey had just finished moving, finally settled in, and asked me to come over for dinner. I didn't think twice about coming over; and the fact I have been lounging around being anti-social towards everyone, it was time for me to get up out the house. He texts me the address and I hop out the bed, make my way towards the shower.

Let the night begin.

I pull up to a high tower building downtown. Just before I could tell him I was here my phone vibrates with a text.

Text: Valet park room 626.

For some reason I was feeling like I probably underdressed. I had on an all-black Nike jogging outfit with wheat tims; my hair tied up looking super comfy.

It was still wintertime so getting dressed up was definitely out of the question. Besides, it wasn't like we were actually going out to dinner; we were staying inside.

As he slightly jogged towards my car, valet opens my door.

"Good evening ma'am are you overnight parking?"

"No…. just going to be here for a few hours."

"May I have the room number and last name on the room."

"Jenkins room 626" with a slight giggle. I thought it was kind of cute how I still remembered his last name.

While assisting me out of the car I reach into my purse to grab a few dollar bills.

"Thank you" proceeding to hand Valet a tip for his kind gesture.

I usually do not tip valet service until I leave, but there was something about his energy and how welcoming he was.

Smiling. "Appreciate it ma'am. Thank you very much you have a nice night.

"Thanks. You do the same."

Valet awaits me at the door.

Making my way to the elevator. I began talking to myself. I had a habit of doing that for some reason it just made me feel more at ease hearing my own voice.
How do I look? Nervously fixing my hair and adjusting my clothes using the elevator as a mirror.

Ding!

The elevator doors open, and I get in and I press the sixth floor. As I was exiting the elevator, I start to get nervous. This lightweight reminded me of how me and my girls would do bachelor parties at hotels, standing at the door debating on who is going to knock and walk in first. It was so childish yet funny.

I mean imagine you are about to dance in front of a group of people half naked and you have to be the first person to walk in. But there was no debate tonight I was knocking on the door and walking in first.

I take a deep breath and knock. Slightly opening the door Stacey greets me with this huge ass smile. If I would remember anything, I will remember those deep dimples. His smile was priceless.

I proceeded to walk in. Before moving any further, I take my shoes off. Something about people walking around the house in the same shoes they have been walking around the streets in did not sit well with me. If I do not do it at my house, I'm not going to do it at nobody else's.

"Wassup stranger?" he said embracing me with a firm hug.

"Nah you the stranger." I jokingly replied.

The scent of his cologne lingered as we hugged. As I was making my way to his bar stool; I was not trying to be *too* nosy, but still checking out the place. It was nice clean and beautifully decorated.

I absolutely loved his kitchen, from all the cabinet space to the big ass marble island countertop. I enjoyed cooking so I can imagine cooking a nice as meal in this kitchen. It was the fact he was making dinner that was very impressive. I cannot remember the last time a man cooked me a meal. I am usually the one always cooking.

"Shit, for real I just finished school for radio and Broadcasting. Graduating in two weeks. Super excited about that."

Attending to the boiling water on the stove, but still engaged in the conversation he responded, "Awwww shit Congratulations.... that's wassup. How was it?"

"I really learned a lot. I thought radio was my thing because I enjoy music, like to talk, and have a good personality. But I got more into filming, directing, and editing. Which was so different because I did not have to be seen or heard yet I could still be creative. I'm raw as fuck with a dope ass imagination." I said laughing.

I slightly paused as I was trying not to talk too much. He takes his focus off of the stove to give me direct eye contact.

"That's wassup. So, what's next?"

"I'm not completely sure. But I am definitely considering writing a book. I stay with some good ass stories. Then who knows, I'll start doing movies too."

"That's raw and a dope idea. What you gonna do to celebrate?"

"I don't really have nothing planned."

Shockingly surprised he responded, "Nahhhh this a special day you should be doing something to celebrate."

As proud as I was of myself on such an accomplishment, I was not big on celebrating. I guess because throughout the last 8 months of school I have only vented to Jason about everything.

I mean every now and then I will talk to my friends and family about school, but Jason was the main person. And now that we are on bad terms, I guess the celebration felt a little different.

We were only allowed three tickets for graduation. That was annoying because I wanted my favorite sister, mother, Jason and 4 of my closest friends to be there.

I had my best friend CJ reach out to Jason to see if he would come and he said he was not coming. I hated the fact that Jason was so stubborn. Like we have been through way worse and you just can't let it go?

"Like real shit Jazz this an accomplishment you should be somewhere out of town celebrating." He said walking towards the cabinet he opens the door and pull out a bottle of 1942.

"And we're about to drink to your accomplishment." He continued pouring up two fat ass shots we toast.

I can't even lie, he made me feel so good and proud of myself. This was the type of energy I needed. This didn't seem like a big deal to me but the fact I had the right people around me to show me it was made a huge difference.

"So wassup, where we going?"

I begin to spin around on the stool looking up at the ceiling thinking to myself. *Where would you want to go?*

"Miami!" I whispered.

I loved Miami. The water, weather, food, music, clubs. The whole vibe was crazy. Plus, it was cold as fuck in Cleveland right now and I could use a tan and kick it.

"Shit Miami sounds good." I said.

"We going to Miami then. I'm booking it tomorrow." He replied with no hesitation.

"Alright bet." I said smirking.

I was not sure if he was bullshitting or not and I wasn't about to question it either. Because whether he was serious or not, I knew *I* was going but it would be nice to go with him though.

"What you over there cooking?"

"You gotta wait 'til I fix your plate to see." he jokingly replied.

An hour goes by and we're 3 blunts in and half a bottle of 1942 down. Dinner is finally ready, smothered chicken breast, homemade mashed potatoes, and asparagus. I was extremely impressed. From the presentation to the fact this man actually cooked a nice ass dinner. Jason has never made me dinner; shit he has never made me a damn sandwich. He works every day all day, so I am usually the one at home cooking. Which was no problem at all because I really enjoy cooking. But every now and then it would have been nice to get the same in return.

It was getting kind of late, before heading out I washed the dishes. He insisted that I didn't have to, but I wanted to, and it really wasn't a problem at all.

I had a thirty-minute drive home. And honestly that 1942 started to have my pussy throbbing. Having self-control is particularly important. Besides, we'll be in Miami, soon right?

"Dinner was great. I think it's raw you know how to cook."

"Thank you. Growing up in a household full of women you tend to learn a lot. Especially cooking."

I begin to gather my things together and make my way towards the door.

Drifting my attention back to Stacey, "Thanks

again for dinner."

"No problem at all. Let me know you made it in safe."

We both embrace one last hug this was more aggressive, and a slight kiss came right after. Deep down inside I wanted his tongue down my throat and his hands gripping my ass.

Once again, self-control.

"Goodnight."

The following morning, I wake up to a text:
About to book these flights send full name and address.

Rolling over in bed, sun beaming through the blinds with a huge smile on my face, *damn this nigga not playing. He literally booked the flights and trip the next day. That's the type of energy I'm talking about!*

What's crazy is I still haven't heard from this nigga Jason. When we were beefing, we would go days even weeks without speaking to each other. He really would ignore my texts and miss my calls.

I'm talking block me off all social media. I wasn't used to that kind of relationship. But it's like I settled for it because that's how he acted. I'm used to communicating and talking out my problems not just ignoring them then coming back around like nothing happened.

What's worse is even when he was wrong, I was always the one reaching out to make things right. I had such a soft spot for him not just because I loved him but because I believe life is too short to hold meaningless grudges. I rather be loving on you then arguing with you; rather talk our problems out instead of acting like they are not there. But at the same time, I was getting to the point where if my effort isn't being matched, I shouldn't be around it. I want to feel like he cares. Effort is so important to me and he was not giving me that.

I kind of contemplated on this because I was not expecting Stacey to book the tickets so fast. I thought he was possibly talking shit but clearly, he wasn't.

Then what if Jason did come to my graduation? That won't change the fact we haven't talked in a month but once I tell him I'm going to Miami there goes another problem. I call my girl Tresse before I decide to reply to Stacey text.

"Bitchhhhhhhhhhh!" I yelled.

"Ohhhhhhhh lord what's the tea?" Sounding so interested in what I was about to tell her.

One thing about me I stay with a story. So, she knew this was something juicy.

Letting out a loud ass laugh. "Bitch! So, why I went over Stacey house for dinner last night and we were catching up. So, I mentioned the fact that I graduate in a week from school and he asked what I was doing to celebrate. I told him nothing really. Long story short the nigga wanna take me to Miami and he literally just texted me for my info to book my flight."

"Damnnnn he raw for that. Real nigga shit. So, I know you're going right?"
Letting out a slight sigh. "Man shit I want to go. It's not like he's some new nigga either so I'm definitely going to be comfortable and I could really use the trip dead ass."

"Let me guess. You tripping on going cause of Jason?" sarcastically speaking.

Smacking my lips. "Bitch yes! I haven't even talked to the nigga just kind of worried about if he actually shows up. Like what if we get back cool? Going to Miami is about to be another argument."

"Jazz you deserve to go. Real shit. I know you love and care about Jason but that nigga not trying to take you out of town."

Tresse had no filter when it came to speaking on how she felt. That's why she's always the first person I call when I have a dilemma.

"And not saying that just because a nigga takes you out of town, he's better than the next. I'm just saying this is a big accomplishment in your life. And for someone to want to do something special for you FOR ONCE I say BITCH GO!"

Laughing, "Huhhhhhhhh I hate shit like this."

"Shit like what?"

Propping myself on my pillow getting more comfortable, "Overthinking and not knowing how a nigga feel. Like I know me and Jason beefing but to go out of town with a nigga and he find out about it."

I let out a huge sigh.

"Man bye! You ain't heard from Jason and bitch you ain't about to sit around and wait." She slightly paused. "He can't be mad at you for doing what you want and he's not even speaking to you. Your life don't run on his time so stop acting like it."

Sitting on the edge of the bed knees to my chest feet on the bed rail I'm really going back and forth in my head on what to do.

"Go Jazz!" Tresse demanded.

Deep down I wanted to go. And I honestly deserved it. Tresse was right. I haven't talked to Jason and my life doesn't go on hold for anyone. I mean he's doing ok with not speaking to me, right?

If he cared, he would have been reached out by, now right? If the shoe were on the other foot, he probably would have done the same right?

Exhaling my breath, "Yeahhhh bitch I'm going."

"Yesssssss bitcccchhhh and don't feel bad about it

either!"

I hop out the bed open my blinds and crack the window. This conversation done got me energized and ready to start my day. It is sunny yet chilly and it's the middle of November nothing but heavy wind and leaves all over the ground.

Taking my focus back to the phone. "Alright girl let me send him this info over. Don't forget Drew party is this Saturday."

"Yeah, thirsty you ain't gone let me forget. Love you see you Saturday."

"Love you more see you later."

Drew was another nigga I was fucking with. We have been messing around for almost six years. I've been in three relationships since knowing him. You can pretty much say he was my side nigga.

He stood 6'2, brown clear skin, low fade with the perfect waves, chinky eyes that showed his little gap in between his teeth every time he smiled.

He was very athletic, so his body was toned and muscular. I am talking looking at him naked would get my pussy so wet. His body was so damn perfect. Even his ass was nice. I've never even noticed or cared about a man's ass 'til I seen his.

The sex was amazing, took me to ecstasy. Whatever fantasy I had he was willing to make come true and I was willing to do whatever as well. Made me feel so nasty and like a freak ass bitch.

After sex I always wanted more. I felt like a whole ass porn star when it came to that dick. I'm talking all holes go, fuck me wherever, use toys, threesomes, foursomes, record me, nut wherever you want sex. My pussy craved him. Not only did he satisfy my sexual urges but, he absolutely respected my lifestyle. A lot of men can't handle women dancing. Although we were not in a relationship he not once ever threw this stripping shit in my face. I'm talking from when I go to work, have a booking, anything involving me getting to the money he was supportive. He would always tell me to have a great night and would wake up in the morning asking me how my night was.

That really mattered to me. He always made me feel like I could be *me*. Very accepting to a lot of things most men wouldn't be. I had no reason to lie to him and most times no need to explain myself to him, but I did.

Furthermore, he was an amazing father. Very interactive with his kids and I absolutely thought that was one of the most attractive things about him.

From training, attending games, helping with homework, being so active with all three of them. Family was important to me. I was the same way with my family especially my sisters and nieces.

Drew's birthday was coming up and he was throwing a party at a venue this Saturday. I usually don't miss work, but I didn't mind taking a night off for him. He's been at every birthday celebration of mine, so I was definitely going to be there for his.

Although we had this great relationship there were still faults. He was quiet which was so different for me. Like he was an exceptionally good listener and speaker but more so on my situations.

If I were going through something, I'd reach out to him and he'd get me together. But I did not feel like he was as open to me. To get to know him was like interrogating him.

He was not affectionate at all, just so damn chill and laid back. Weird but it was still ok because what he lacked, I got elsewhere.

I just really love that he fucked me good, treated me ok and accepted me for being me. He had bitches for sure and I may have been his favorite but that holds no weight if he still has to go elsewhere. Deep down I wanted more but at the same time I like where we stood.

Attending back to my phone I text Stacey my info.

Bet he replied.

Thank you I appreciate it. ☐

No problem you deserve it.

Looking at those words *You deserve it* put a huge smile on my face. There is nothing like someone acknowledging your accomplishments. It felt good as fuck. Whether Jason and I got back talking or not Miami was a go for sure: booked and ready, no turning back.

Graduation Day

I was so excited about graduating today. Although I had my High School diploma, I never got to experience walking across stage in a cap and gown with friends and family cheering me on.

This was such a big deal. We were only allowed to invite three guests, but I invited four of my closest friends, including Tresse, my mom, favorite sister, and Drew.

I was kind of nervous about Drew attending only if Jason were to miraculously appear. How awkward would that be?

Then again, how selfish would that be of me not to share such an accomplishment with someone who wants to be there for me?

I took home two trophies. One for *Best Video Project* and another for *Outstanding Work in TV Arts*. I was so proud of myself and I just knew this was only the beginning. I absolutely loved writing and filming. I really can see myself as the next Tyler Perry. My imagination is so amazing. The creativity within me stands out.

Suddenly I had an epiphany. As happy as I was to have some of the people I love around during this celebration, the fact Jason didn't show, call or text bothered me. Me really calling him a bitch ass nigga made him miss out on a day so special to *me?*

He couldn't put it to the side and be there for me?

Not a call.

Not a text.

Absolutely nothing.

The thing is had it been me I would have showed, probably would not have spoken to him but I would have been there on a day that meant so much to him.

I am just a firm believer that life is too short and certain things you cannot get back and time is one of them.

Jason should have been there no excuse!

I quickly snapped out of it!

What matters right now is those who are here.

They support you.

They love you.

They are proud of you.

If Jason wanted to be there, he would've. Don't ruin your day.

I wore a plaid dress that flourished out at the bottom. My hair was in a platinum blonde bob. Tan open toes with the chunky heel shoes. Dranice did my makeup. I was looking as beautiful as ever.

My cap was so dope. My tattoo artist DB designed it for me. The visual was a girl upside down on the pole while another girl was filming her with the saying *From Pole to Goals*. I thought the concept was very dope and described me so well. Showing myself and especially other entertainers that dancing is not your only art. Use the money you make to invest in your future. You cannot dance forever.

At the end of the ceremony everyone gathered in the hall. I instantly noticed Drew. Looking fine as ever, dressed in an all-black Nike suit with some all-red LeBron 17's.

It is so weird how I will fuck and suck the soul out of him, yet his presence still made me feel nervous and quite shy. Making my way towards him I greet him with a smile and a tight ass hug. Started to grab his dick but I chilled.

"I seen you getting all the awards."

Giggling, "Yeahhhhh man I really worked my ass off. I'm so happy."

"As you should. I'm proud of you girl."

While soaking in all the good energy I hear someone call my name.

"Jazzzzzzzz let me get a pic with you and your friends." my sister insisted.

As everyone gathered to take a picture, I grab Drew's hand letting him follow my lead. We don't have too many pictures together and if so, it's usually some freak shit or some off guards.

He was getting in this picture, it wasn't no standing to the side, *you're* by my side. We all pull together as my sister captures this moment. It felt good having so much support around me, my weekend was about to be crazy. Drew's birthday party then next week I'm catching a flight to Miami.

Life's Great!

Drew's Party

I was at the house getting ready for Drew party. Standing in the mirror I am admiring how fine I look. This black one piece showed all my curves. The top was lace so I put a black bra underneath. My breast sat up so perfectly. Stomach slightly showing and the red *Jessica Simpson's* pumps made me go from 5'8 to 6'2.

The long deep wavy hair to my shoulders complimented my face. Dranice came through and did my makeup. I'm not really heavy on makeup unless it is a special occasion. I don't even wear the shit at work. I was pulling tight tonight. Tresse was finishing up getting dressed she was going to meet me there.

I pull up to the venue and surprisingly Tresse beat me there. My bitch was looking so good. Tresse was shorter than me she had to be at least 5'3 and in heels about 5'7. Bitch always made me look huge when we went out. She was wearing this cute ass skin tight all red dress with some black pumps.

"Yesssssssss bitch!" she yelled in excitement.

Cheesing hard I yell back, "Bitchhhhhh you looking real good tonight!"

Laughing. We embrace each other with a hug then begin making our way inside.

"Girl I need a drink; I had a long ass day at work. Couldn't wait to get off. Shit so damn draining it ain't even funny."

Tresse was a RN at Cleveland Clinic. Barely had time to kick it and when she wanted to, I always had to work. I just don't see myself missing work to go to a regular club get drunk and spend money when I can go to work dance get money and get drunk. It would have to be a special occasion for me to miss out on some money, especially on the weekends.

Drew was worth me missing a bag. I'll get it back.

"First round on me."

The venue was beautiful. Very grown and sexy vibes. Chris Brown and Usher remix *Back to Sleep* was playing as we entered. The women were dressed in classy outfits. The men were looking like fine gentlemen. The whole vibe was so cool and relaxing.

The dance floor was huge, and the outside was surrounded by tables and chairs. Very spacious. Food was also being served. I hated going to parties with no food. Being drunk and hungry don't feel good. A bitch be ready to go all because I want something to eat. The whole set up was just nice and well put together. Drew did this thing.

Heading towards the open bar I noticed one bartender in particular name Shay who was serving drinks and she happened to be Stacey's ex-girlfriend. I've seen her around the city plenty of times and she bartended at a strip club I was working at.

The only time we spoke was when I was ordering drinks otherwise, we had nothing to talk about. She recently went viral for fighting over him. Bitch got beat up by a hoe name Ari. By the looks of the video, it really wasn't a fair fight. Ari snuck up on her did some sucka shit. But who is to say what is a fair fight or not? The bitch probably deserved it.

It happened before Stacey and I made plans on going to Miami, but I found out about it afterwards. Otherwise, I probably would have reconsidered going with all the drama he got going on. I am a chill type chick. I don't do no arguing or fighting over any man. It is amazing how one man can bring you a handful of mad bitches.

And what a coincidence it just so happened to be her birthday. That is all she kept yelling. All the other bartenders were taking orders, so she was the only one available.

"Hey what y'all drinking?

"Hey, let me get a double of Hennessy and a double of Avion. Two bottles of water too."

Before going to make our drinks, I tell her to grab

herself something as well. I always offered bartenders drinks, I'm sure their ass be needing it.

Although, I knew I would be in Miami with her ex real soon it was the kind gesture and me just being the person I am. She is not my friend, so I don't owe her shit. She comes back with all our drinks.

"Thank you" as she brings her cup to toast to ours.

"Happpppppyyyyy Birthdayyyyyyyyy!" slightly singing in unison.

Chugging her drink down she gathers our cups proceeding to walk towards another group of ladies who had a drink waiting for her.

Just when I was making my way to the dance floor the group yells out, "Miamiiiiiiiiiiiiiii next weekend!"

I stopped dead in my tracks looked at Tresse. Glancing over to confirm she heard what I heard but, she was too busy in her phone trying to take a selfie.

"Bitcccccchhhh did you just hear that?" I asked.

Taking her attention off the phone, "Nah what?"

"Dude I'm not tripping they dead ass said Miami next weekend. "

We stood there for a few moments and they say it again.

"Bitchhhh you ain't tripping they dead ass just said they're going to Miami. You think that nigga booked y'all trip on the same weekend on purpose?"

"Hell nah we planned this two weeks prior and I'm the one who suggested Miami not him and I chose the dates."

"Girl what a fucking coincidence."

"Man what? What if we are on the same flight together? What if we stay in the same hotel? This is about to be so fucking awkward dude."

I can't even lie I'm just thinking in my head this is not about to be right. But I wasn't worried about shit. We are going on this trip and we're going to have a good time.

"Are you going to tell him about her going the same weekend too?" Tresse asked.

"I'll talk to him about it later. I'm sure he probably doesn't even know. I've been around him a lot lately, she's been blowing him up since that damn fight and he's been ignoring her."

"Yeah, I seen that shit on Instagram. So messy. I'll never understand why bitches fight over these niggas." Tresse adds.

"Sometimes it's not even the nigga, it's the disrespect. You know social media make a lot of bitches feel tough."

"Oh well! It is what it is. Miami about to be going. We need another drink 'cause I can tell now that your trip about to be crazy and as always you're going to have a story to tell."

Grabbing us another round this time I sip my drink instead of downing it. Tonight, was about Drew all this extra shit can wait.

As I'm making my way back to the dance floor, I noticed Drew walking in. I just couldn't take my eyes off him. Greeting his guest, I admired the Checker London Fog Fur collar jacket he wore, complimenting the floral and black button down underneath. Gray Tommy Hilfiger slacks with a Gucci belt. Some all-black Giorgio Armani shoes to top it off. Low top fade with the waves. Gucci shades hiding his dark brown eyes. I was ready to hop on his dick the moment I seen him. His presence always made me nervous yet excited.

The night was amazing everybody had a good time. After leaving the party I was expecting Drew to hit me up, but I didn't hear from him. I could only imagine how many of his bitches came, this nigga had options. But he definitely made it clear on his Instagram that he had other plans.

Goofy nigga posted his bed with rose petals spelling out, *LET ME SUCK YOUR DICK* with balloons that spelt out his name. Shit lightweight annoyed me, had me feeling like I could have gone to work if I wasn't leaving with you afterwards.

I wanted some dick, and I was lightweight drunk. Then again, I couldn't really be too mad. This isn't a relationship and I be doing me too.

For Jason birthday I wore lingerie, lit over 30 candles making a pathway, rose petals all over the floor, with a bed full of birthday gifts and posted it on my page.

I don't know if he was trying to be petty, but it was cool bitch wasn't topping me. I'll fuck him later. Besides, I was about to be in Miami showing my ass with another nigga anyway.

Keep it playa!

I woke up the following morning with a slight hangover. All I wanted was chipotle. That was my go-to for whenever I was super hungover that was the only thing that could bring me back to life. Chipotle to me is what spinach is to Popeye's. Rolling over to check my phone there is a text from Stacey.

"Morning how was your night?"

I kind of wanted to wait to speak on the whole situation with his ex-going on the same trip as us but figured I would bring it up now. We are leaving in a few days and it makes sense to tell him what is going on. I wasn't going to bring it up through text so FaceTime him.

"Morning…. Morning" he answered.

I couldn't help but to smile seeing him standing in the kitchen in nothing but some Versace briefs. Skin looking so chocolate and smooth.

"Mawninnnnnn what you doing?"

Walking back over to the camera he flashes the red coffee mug I bought back for him while I was in Jamaica.

Laughing, "Coffee time huh?"

"Yo' ass the one that got me into drinking this shit."

"Oh really? It's my fault huh?

"I didn't start drinking coffee until you came around. Then you turn around and go buy me a coffee maker with a box of coffee." He said attending back to his coffee. I adjust my pillows take a slight breath and get ready to bring last night up.

"Sooooooo.... about my night.... It was cool but kind of awkward tho'."

Taking his focus off the coffee he comes towards the camera and makes eye contact as if this must be a serious conversation. I kind of rather he kept fucking with the coffee because now I'm lightweight nervous that I have his full attention.

"Why is that?"

"Long story short the party I went to last night

Shay was bartending there. Me and my bitch overheard her say that she was going to Miami next weekend. Which was a coincidence because we are about to be there. I was just wondering did you know anything about it?"

Smacking his lips in disbelief. "Hell, nah I don't talk to that girl. Shit we could've went anywhere you said you wanted to go to Miami so that was the move."

Feeling a little relieved. "Yeah. That's exactly what I told my girl. Not as if I thought that you would do something like that. "

"Man, I don't fuck with that girl. We gone go down there and have a good ass time. This trip about you."

The way he was talking just made my pussy wet. Straight clarification no beating around the bush. We haven't even fucked yet, didn't even know what the dick was hitting for, what it smelt like, how'd it taste, how'd it fit. I know for a fact I was going to find out in Miami.

Airport

Our flight was leaving out at 2:45 and I still hadn't completely finished packing. I don't know why I tend to pack last minute but it always worked for me. I gathered all my things making sure I had everything. Anything I forgot I can get down there.

Grabbing my phone, I look up an Uber to come and get me.

The airport was no further than 15 minutes from me. I made it 10 minutes before 2. Surprisingly, it wasn't too packed, getting through was a breeze. After making my way through security I head towards Gate B15.

As I'm walking, I see Stacey sitting at the bar with his best friend Fat Boy. Fat Boy had a lil' bitch in Miami who he was linking with. Nigga wasn't bringing sand to the beach.

"Yooooooo" slightly hugging Stacey from the back, as I snuck a kiss to his left cheek.

"Yoooooooo we out this bitchhhhhhh" Fat Boy yelled as he looked back to give me a hug.

"Sup what you drinking?" Stacey asked.

As I admired the fresh haircut, he had along with those pretty ass dimples, "Double of Hennessy with a side of coke."

"My nigga you need a chaser?" Fat Boy questioned.

"Hell yeah…. I'm not drinking that shit straight."

"Awwwwww pussssssyyyyyyy"

"Fuck you" slightly slapping his head while raising my drink to toast.

"Cheers! To a great fucking weekend." I yelled.

"Also! Cheers to you for graduating" Stacey said as he chugged down his drink.

That right there made me pause. For that to be the reason why we're even going out of town and I didn't even mention me graduating yet he did, made me feel so good.

Making eye contact I give him a slight grin. "Yeah this shit about to go" I said to myself.

Just as I was starting to gaze into my own little dream world, I hear a group of bitches talking super loud, it totally distracted me. And what do you know it just so happens to be Shay friends. A few of them follow me on social networks.

A couple of them came over spoke to us and kept it moving. She was nowhere in sight, but it was only a matter of time. What a fucking coincidence I clearly said something like this would happen. It's like I really spoke it into existence.

There was no doubt in my mind that we all were on the same flight. I wasn't worried. I knew nothing was about to pop off at the airport let alone on a plane. I just knew nobody better not have said shit to me.

Shay eventually gets there, and we are all at the same bar but within distance. I'm sitting between Stacey and Fat Boy, so you really don't know which one I'm with.

That was the funny part because I can tell by how they were looking that they were trying to figure it out. It was just about time for us to board our flight, so we head over to our section. Just as we are walking there's an announcement that our flight has been delayed two hours.

"Damn two hours?" I said in disbelief.

As much as I hated flight delays, I always thought it was probably a sign from God. Maybe He is protecting us from something happening. Not even just necessarily the flight but even the destination we are heading to. I am a deep thinker I tend to see the good and the bad.

Before we could even get back to the bar our seats were taken. Instead, we sit at a 3 seated table by our departure gate.

I'm sitting next to Stacey talking and Fat Boy is sitting across from us scrolling through his phone. Three of Shays friends walk by and within seconds turn back around. I noticed one of them hoes had their phone out pretending as if she was on it, but I knew she had to be recording us.

How corny are these hoes?

"Aye them hoes ain't never just walk by recording us" I said.

"Man get the fuck out of here. Really?" Fat Boy looking back to see where they are at.

Chuckling. "Shit them hoes so childish. That's

another reason I had to leave the bitch alone." Stacey chimed in.

These two hours couldn't come by fast enough.

Finally, it was time to board our flight. And of course, they were on the same one. We begin lining up. Shay and I made eye contact for a good ten seconds. Nothing was said with the mouth but if her eyes could have talked. I purposely stand closer to Stacey to make it known we are together. Walking down the aisle we have to walk pass them hoes to get to our seat.

"Nigga wearing the shoes I bought him" Shay said indirectly as her friends laughed loudly.

Laughing it off Stacey kept walking.
I give Shay a slight grin and proceed to follow right behind Stacey. She was salty. I could tell deep down inside she wanted to flip on him, but that shit wasn't about to happen. Whether it is because she wants to enjoy her birthday or don't want to get kicked off the plane wasn't shit gone pop off. Especially with me being there.

The approximate flight time from Cleveland Ohio to Miami Florida is three hours and twenty-two minutes. Stay in your seats and keep your seatbelt fastened the flight attendant announces. I wasn't sure how this flight was going to go but I'm ready to takeoff.

Just before taking off I check my Instagram. I'm

going through my messages and come across a DM saying someone posted me in the airport. I click on the video and sure enough it is me and Stacey sitting down talking. I *knew* them bitches were recording us.

"Look...I told you." leaning over towards Stacey to show him the video.

"Them hoes might be on the same flight as us, but they damn sho' not staying where we staying." Stacey laughed.

Then to top it off they are talking shit about how Ari fought Shay over Stacey, but he is on a flight with me. As if Shay don't look just as dumb.

I could have said something to them, but I just know this trip was about to be so bomb. One thing I have mastered is ignoring people. Nothing but positive energy.

Stacey was right. They definitely weren't staying where we were staying. After we get off the plane we're not even gonna see them. Worse scenario we will have to catch the same flight back. The plane begins to move.

Fuck it.

Miami we are on our way!

Miami

Our flight was actually cool.

For some reason I always tend to get lightheaded when a plane land. I was so tired of sitting on my ass I could not wait to stand up. And I definitely couldn't wait to get off this plane and away from these loud ass hoes.

The whole flight all they did was talk. I can't even tell you what they were saying because I put headphones on.

Stacey slept the whole flight. That nigga must have had a long night. Retrieving our luggage, we come across Shay and her friends one last time. Her little bald head friend just could not keep her eyes off of us. And *she's* the one that posted the video.

Deep down inside I'm laughing at her too because I used to fuck on her baby daddy. Use to be squirting all over that dick she was pressed about. It was good but not good enough to be a nigga fifth...six...baby mama.

Sigh, "Weak hoes." I said as we grab our things and head to the exit.

I began to text my peoples that we made it safe. Just as I'm texting my best friend CJ, I open a text that he forward to me. It was from Jason. Shay texted him.

Shay: What's the odds your ex and my ex are out of town together on my birthday? lol.

Jason: My Ex?

Shay: Temptation

Jason: Lol

Shay: I just died.

Shay: We all on the same flight

Jason: He can have her.

Shay: She can have him.

I knew this would happen. I already knew Jason would find out especially if we were all on the same flight, I just didn't think she would text him.

Like how this dusty bitch even have his number?

And why is he texting my best friend when he could have texted me?

Straight pussy.

And what does he mean Stacey can have me? Like I'm some toy. I haven't spoke to the nigga in Damn near two months. He didn't show call or text for my graduation.

Stacey had me the moment he asked me what I wanted to do to celebrate. I definitely didn't care how Jason felt. I mean why should I? I was going to enjoy the trip even more now.

WE IN MIAMI BITCCCHHHHHHH!

Stacey booked us a room at The Fontainebleau. As many times as I've been to Miami I've never stayed here.

Scenic ocean views and six outdoor swimming

pools surrounded by private cabanas. A night club, nine restaurants and a spa.

Our suite was absolutely amazing. We had a full kitchen, living room, bathroom with the jacuzzi tub inside. Walking onto the patio I admired the beautiful ocean, along with the palm trees and pools.

Such an amazing view. And the fact we were staying on the twenty-fifth floor made it even more lit. He was absolutely right them bitches definitely wasn't staying here.

"You like?" coming from behind hugging me from the back and placing a slight kiss on my neck.

Turning towards him I wrap my arms around his neck. "It's beautiful." Pulling him closer and tonguing him down slowly.

Taking both of his hands gripping my ass while spreading my cheeks apart he gives me tongue back. I could feel his dick slightly gliding along my thigh. I take my hand and begin caressing his shaft through his sweatpants. It had to be at least nine inches and it was so fucking thick. Just as I was about to get on my knees and place his dick down my throat, there is a knock at the door. More than likely, it was the bellman with our luggage.

"Damn" I sigh in disappointment. I was so ready to suck some dick. "I'll go answer it." I said giggling.

There was no way he was going to the door with a hard on. I wanted some dick, but I was just as ready to get dressed and go out. It is cool we still have all night.

I am ready to drink, smoke, get dressed and have a good time. As the bellman brings our luggage in, I grab my phone and begin to scroll through my Instagram.

Of course, the views were going crazy. I swear negative news travel so fast. I was up to nine thousand views in six hours. And Shay was all up in my shit. I love that Instagram let you know who is viewing your story. And me being me I definitely went to Shay page.

"Yeah bitch! I wanna look too."

Of course, there were nothing but indirect post. Them at the airport and on the plane. Shay trying to clown Ari about looking stupid over Stacey. And from the looks of her background, they were at a regular ass hotel.

Hopefully, they had more than one room it was like six of them. Tossing my phone to the side to bring my attention to the bellman.

"Enjoy your stay ma'am." I reach in my purse and grab a handful of singles.

"Thank you, ma'am."

"No thank you," I insisted as I walked with him towards the door.

"Have a nice night."

Closing the door behind him. I grab our luggage and bring it to the bedroom. Stacey was on the patio talking on the phone. It was going on midnight. Back at home everything closes around two, you start getting dressed at midnight you might as well stay home. The clubs stayed open late out here, I'm talking six in the morning. I begin unpacking my things, trying to figure out what I am wearing tonight.

"Fat Boy about to grab a bottle of Hen you want anything else?"

"Nah I'm good! Thanks."

Going through my luggage I began pulling clothes out figuring what am I going to wear tonight. I brought this snakeskin one-piece pants fit that complimented my figure so well.

I'm talking showed all my curves, damn near look painted on. Strings in the front that laced up crisscross, so I had control on how my breast sat up. Stomach slightly showing. Topped it off with some 5inch Steve Madden open toe black heels.

I wore black shoulder length wavy hair, with a slight part showing some forehead. As much as I hated my forehead, I actually liked the style and after putting on some makeup I liked it even more. It complimented my entire face from my big nostrils, nicely shaped eyebrows, long eyelashes, big full lips, caramel skin.

I wasn't the best at doing my make up, but I thought I was pretty OK. I literally do my make up in less than

10 minutes and with like 3 brushes. One thing I can say is that Jason used to compliment me on doing it myself.

I would rather go to a professional and get it done and sometimes he would think it was too much. I just always felt like it wasn't enough when I used to do it. I appreciated the compliment but on a special occasion I am definitely going to my makeup artist. I figured I would start getting dressed I'm sure I'll take longer than him.

I was looking so damn good. Admiring myself in the mirror as Pandora played Neyo's, "Miss Independent." I was so ready to kick it. Just as I begin putting on my lipstick Stacey comes in the bathroom. Before I could even compliment how handsome he looked, he got me first.

"You look real nice," he said as he hugged me from behind making eye contact through the mirror.

We looked good as fuck together. The way he just embraced me made my pussy feel like it had a heartbeat. I hate that I always find myself comparing certain things to Jason, but I can't recall not one time I've ever gotten dressed at Jason 's house let alone him complimenting me on how nice I looked when I did go out. He just seems like he always had some type of animosity towards me going out and about especially if I was a dressed up. And the fact that I barely went out I could not understand why he wasn't as supportive as I wanted him to be.

"You look just as good baby."

Slightly pausing. There is a knock on the door.

"That must be Fat Boy," he said making his way to the door I began to reapply the gloss on my lips from kissing him.

"SHOOOOOOOOOOOOT TIMMMMMMMEEEEE!" a female voice yelled.

"Yesssssssssssssssssssss!" I yelled back.

Not too sure who she was I haven't even seen her yet but was totally loving the energy already. I was so ready to turn up and she seem to be on the same page.
Adjusting my outfit, I make my way to the kitchen.
Fat Boy and Stacey was getting ready to roll up as ole girl began pouring shots. With her back turned towards me, all I could see was long blonde hair. She couldn't have been no taller than 5'6 and that's with heels on. Slightly chubby but it was proportioned to her height and looked good. Turning around to bring the shots to the kitchen counter.

"Shoooooooooots!" she sang loudly.

Greeting her with a smile. "Heyyyyyyyyyyyyyy shoooooots!" I sang back.

"I'm Asia. You drinking Henny or Patron?"

"Hey Asia, I'm Jazz and I'll do a double double of Hennessy."

"Double? Double?" Stacey jokingly mimicked me.

"Yeah. As a matter of fact, we're all doing double doubles. LET'S GO!" Asia demanded.

Damn I love this bitch energy. She's just like me. Fat Boy sure know how to pick 'em! Asia looked like the typical white girl. Blonde hair, blue eyes, nothing exotic about her.

As much shit as Fat Boy talked, thought he was bringing a Kim Kardashian or some foreign type bitch. One thing for sure I knew she had to have money. She looks like the type that cake niggas and if that is what she did trust me Fat Boy was all in. I ain't knock it. Women do that shit to men all the time.

I raise both of my shots in the air as everyone else followed along. "Toast to a good fucking night. We in Miammmmmiiiiiiiiii let's make the best of it and we're taking both of these doubles RIGHT NOW."

Bringing our shots in to toast, we down one double then down the other. "Aight let's roll."

Gathering our things, we make our way to the door.

Time to party!

PARTY TIME

Club LIV was going so hard. One of the hottest clubs and hardest clubs to get into in Miami and it was literally downstairs from us. By us staying at The Fontainebleau there was no cover charge. It was huge. I'm talking upstairs and down. This wasn't no T-shirt, tennis shoes type of kick it. Everyone was dressed up. Grown and sexy vibes. And the best part we can smoke weed inside.

"Wanna get a bottle? "Stacey asked.

Although we had liquor in the room of course we couldn't bring it to the club.

"Shit we can." I said walking towards the bar as I grab the drink menu on the counter.

"Damn $450 for a bottle of Hennessy?"

"Shit sound crazy but we are in Miami" Stacey trying to make it make sense.
One thing about me I don't believe in spending unnecessary money. I know Stacey didn't care about the price, but I did. Not only that but shit we have the same thing upstairs.

"Nah. How about we just get two double doubles each. I mean how much liquor do we need? We're a double double in already."

"You sure?"

"Yup we'll be good."

98

Grabbing the waitress attention, he orders our drinks. Total came up to $200. Twenty-five dollars a shot. I am not a cheapskate, but that's ridiculous. Hennessy shots go for no more than ten bucks at home. But rather spend two hundred dollars than four hundred fifty. And boy did we get our money worth.

I don't know what the hell kind of Hennessy we had but as the night went by and the music played, I felt that shit. Throughout the whole night, I danced my ass off. I couldn't help but to be on Stacey. He was looking just as good as I was feeling. He was so chill admiring me the whole night.

Yelling over the music", Baby you good?" I asked with a slight slur.

And even if he weren't, I wouldn't had been no help. I was just about over it. Feet was killing me to the point the liquor couldn't even help.

"Yeah baby. I'm straight. Need anything else?" he asked.

"Yeah, for you to stop babysitting that drink" I jokingly replied.

"Shit. This some different kind of Hennessy" laughing.

"Man, I swear it is. I'm damn near smacked off two doubles. That's rare as fuck."

"How you feeling?" Stacey asking me that damn near had me instantly say *Ready to fuck*, but I caught myself and just before I could respond the DJ cuts the music down.

"Yoooooooooo" we have a very very special guest in the building ladies and gentlemen. As a matter of fact, we have a few special guests here tonight."

Focusing my attention to the DJs announcement. *Dreams and Nightmare* by Meek Mill begin playing.

"We got mothafuking Meek Mill in the building. "the DJ screamed on the mic.

Trying not to look like a groupie but still get a glance I look up towards the section he was making his way to. With his whole entourage I could barely see him.

He was dressed in all black, chains hanging from his neck, wrist and fingers glistening from the diamonds Meek settled himself into his section. The bottle girls wasted no time. Had to be about fifteen of them and all of them were holding bottles of Ace of Spades. The introduction to *Dreams and Nightmare* alone just gets everyone turnt up. And once Meek hit 'em with the, *Hold up wait a minute I thought y'all was finished* confetti was all over the club.

Before you knew it, Lil Wayne, Trey Songz, 2Chainz, Jamie Foxx and a few other celebrities were in the building. I can't even lie as much fun as I was having my feet were killing me and I was just about ready to go. Stacey was so chill, but I could tell he was just about over it.

"Sup ready to go?" I asked.

"Whenever you're ready baby."

"I'm ready. We can go."

I was so happy our room was right upstairs. My feet were killing me so damn bad. I absolutely hated wearing heels but going out to a club just didn't feel right if I didn't wear them.

Finally, we made it to the room. Slightly stumbling inside as Stacey helped me balance myself. I instantly take my heels off.

With a sigh of relief taking a second to embrace the pleasure of my feet being on the floor. The Hennessy was rushing through me. I was drunk and I was feeling it more than ever now. Proceeding to undress as Stacey stood behind me, I bend over and instantly feel his rock-hard dick gliding along my ass.

Sliding one leg out of my bodysuit I grab his dick from in between my thighs. Slowly stroking him as my ass stayed tooted up. Sliding my other leg out of my suit, I face forward and begin licking the shaft while slowly caressing his balls. He was at least a good nine inches. To top it off it was thick too. I kind of understand why that hoe Shay mad, his dick was not even inside me yet and my pussy was drippin'!

Standing in the kitchen not taking his eyes off me as I'm on my knees devouring every inch, he grabs my face and begin to tongue me down. Then push my face back down to keep sucking then bring my face back up to kiss me again.

My mouth was so wet that the spit from us kissing was dripping all over his dick onto the floor. I wanted to feel every inch down my throat and that I did. As the tears rolled down my face Stacey slightly begins to moan.

I'm rubbing on my pussy as he's holding my face up and fucking my mouth. All you could hear was the splashing of me squirting hitting the floor. Nothing but straight eye contact. Getting off my knees making my way to his lips I slowly put my tongue in his mouth as I begin unbuttoning his shirt. Pants was already down to his ankles. Grabbing his hand, I guide him to the balcony.

The soft breeze that filled the air brushed upon our naked bodies. As I stood over the balcony, he begins massaging my shoulders slowly gliding his tongue along my ear. Usually, my ear is my ticklish spot just breathing close to it have me laughing but this was different. I felt butterflies and chills.

Placing my hands on the rail I bend overlooking back giving Stacey the go. With no hesitation he puts his manhood inside me.

Wow he felt so good.

The thickness of his dick applied pressure, but I know I can take it. Admiring the city view at night on the twenty fifth floor while getting stroked from behind had me at ecstasy. Wrapping one arm around my waist while the other was on my breast he speeds up. I take his hand off my breast and placed it on my throat.

I wanted to be choked.

"Ohhhhh you like being choked huh?"

Pounding harder I take it he took me wanting to be choked meant I wanted rough sex. And that I did. The strokes got harder and my moans got louder.

"Dick good as fukkkkkkkk" I moaned.

I bend over further and spread my ass open as he goes deeper, he begins choking me harder this time both hands around my throat. As I am taking every stroke, I'm enjoying Miami view as well. The city was lit up and the skyline was beautiful. The air breezing along our bodies was so soothing. I could feel my body trembling and I was just about ready to cum then I suddenly stopped.

I wanted to get on top.

Scoping the balcony, I noticed a chair not too far. Grabbing his dick, I guide him to follow me. Before sitting in the chair, I squat down and put him back in my mouth, grabbing his hand and placing it on my head to give him control on how fast he wanted me to go.

Aggressive sex turned me on so much.

Like grab my head and shove your dick down my throat or grab my head and slowly stroke your dick down my throat. Slightly pushing him onto the chair I get on top.

Gasping, "Damn Jazzzz......."

Placing my hand around his neck pushing myself closer to feel him deeper.

"Stacey you feel so fucking good" I returned.

Proceeding to bounce up and down as he spreaded my ass open I could feel myself about to climax.

"Stacey…. Stacey…. baby I'm about to cum."

"Cum all over that dick…. cum all over it."

Rocking my hips back and forth and gripping my pussy muscles in and out my body begins to shiver.

Grabbing my throat "I said cum on this dick" he demanded.

"Right now, baby…right nowwwww." I screamed as he went harder. I was at complete bliss. Feeling his soft, chocolate, smooth skin, and broad shoulders along my body. Admiring his dimples as he licked his lips, the slight gap between his teeth as he bit down on his bottom lip. Although I just came, I was not done. I spin around while still inside me and continue to ride. Grabbing my breast while grinding along with me I begin to climax again.

"Where you want this nut?" he asked.

I'm thinking to myself of course not in me but on me. That could be my ass, my face, mouth. I was feeling freaky as hell and this was our first time ever having sex. Not sure if I wanted to be nasty or nasty nasty.

"All over my ass baby…. I want a fat nut"

Pulling out I feel his warm nut shoot on me. Bouncing my ass as he jacked his dick in between my cheeks I grip his dick. Holding it right between my cheeks as if I'm getting every drip of nut out.

"Damn you got some good ass pussy."

Those words were like music to my ears. Not to toot my own horn I have heard it multiple times and hearing Stacey confirm brought a smile on my face. Started to tell him how amazing the sex was and how good his dick felt in me but did not want to make it seem like I was just returning the compliment. His warm nut drips in between my crack redirecting his focus on my ass.

With a slight tease I walk away, and he follows my lead. Making my way to the bathroom I turn on the shower. I can feel the nut running from my ass down to my thighs. I cannot remember the last time I took a shower with a man, but this felt like *everything*. Our wet bodies touching, he even washed my back for me. Something so simple as that made me feel so good. Calling it a night we make our way to the bed. Cuddling behind me.

"Thank you for everything I really appreciate it. I really didn't care to celebrate me graduating until you made me feel like it was a big accomplishment."

Pulling me closer he says to me, "That's a big accomplishment Jazz. When you told me, you were graduating the excitement you had made me excited. I was surprised that you didn't have plans to celebrate."

Slightly giggling, "Yeah didn't think too much of it. Me just graduating was enough."

"Jazz celebrate ALL of your accomplishments not just SOME."

Damn that was deep, and he was so right. I graduated from High School and never experienced walking across stage. Never experienced my friends and family supporting such an accomplishment with me.

I was rewarded two trophies. And I honestly worked my ass off and enjoyed every bit of it. So, what made me think that it was not a BIG DEAL? Not sure where our relationship was going from here on out, but I needed this energy around me. I needed someone to remind me of my worth and to uplift me. And Stacey was doing just that. He wasn't doing it to get pussy or to tell me what I wanted to hear a nigga really cared and showed it.

"That's deep and real. From here on out I'll make sure I'll do so. I needed to hear that."

Holding me a little tighter he places a kiss on neck. Pushing myself back towards him I feel his manhood poking me right at the top part of my ass. Purposely bringing my ass back forward.

Round two?

This by far was one of the best trips I have ever been on. We had so much fun. Besides the stupid shit before coming Stacey really showed me a good time and I'm sure he had just as good of a time. The flight home was even funnier because Shay and her friends were on that flight as well. And of course, they looked with their eyes and nothing came out their mouths. Although, I knew this trip would come with drama it was so well worth it.

I learned two valuable lessons: Surround yourself with people who motivate and encourage you. Also, celebrate your accomplishments no matter how little they may seem.

ABOUT THE AUTHOR

Jazzminique Mobley was born and raised in Cleveland, Ohio. She is also known as Temptation216, one of the top entertainers in the city.
Jazzminique has always had a passion for writing. She recently graduated from Ohio Media School for Radio and Broadcasting.

Connect with Jazzminique:

Instagram @temptation_216

Twitter @216Temptation

Made in the USA
Middletown, DE
19 March 2021